EDGE
BOOKS™

SPORTS TO THE EXTREME

EXTREME
Water Sports

BY ERIN K. BUTLER

CAPSTONE PRESS
a capstone imprint

Edge Books are published by Capstone Press,
1710 Roe Crest Drive, North Mankato, Minnesota 56003
www.mycapstone.com

Library of Congress Cataloging-in-Publication Data
Library of Congress Cataloging-in-Publication data is available on the Library of Congress website.
ISBN 978-1-5157-7862-2 (library binding)
ISBN 978-1-5157-7866-0 (eBook PDF)

Editorial Credits
Nikki Ramsay, editor; Sara Radka, designer; Laura Manthe, production specialist

Photo Credits
iStockphoto: cover, 1, EpicStockMedia, cover; Shutterstock: Ammit Jack, 20, bikeriderlondon, 19, David Bostock,
9, Dray van Beeck, 25, Dudarev Mikhail, 23, EpicStockMedia, 27, Gail Johnson, 29, GROGL, 21, Kanjanee
Chaisin, 17, Maria Nelasova, 15, Neale Cousland, 11, 13, Neale Cousland, 5, paul prescott, 7, Perspectives/Jeff
Smith, 9, trubavin, 6

Design elements by Book Buddy Media.

The publisher does not endorse products whose logos may appear on objects in images in this book.

Printed in the United States of America.
010364F17

Table of Contents

Extreme Water Sports

Every person needs water — for survival, for power, and for fun. Some people see water as a challenge to overcome. They dive in headfirst, performing incredible feats of bravery and athleticism. Today an entire branch of extreme sports is devoted to Earth's most essential resource.

Water adventurers have been around for centuries. Ancient Egyptians, for example, loved rowing, and even held rowing competitions. People have always tested their limits on the open ocean with activities such as jumping, diving, and surfing. But in recent years, technology has allowed water sports to advance even further. Now people can use specially designed boats, boards, skis, and other watercraft to enter a new frontier. Water has become a playground for extreme athletes.

Whether it is in the ocean, over the rapids of a river, or across a lake, extreme water athletes are able to show off some amazing skills.

EXTREME FACT!

Extreme sports generate about $12.1 billion in sales each year in the United States.

The Czech Republic's Adam Sedlmajer is one of the world's most extreme waterskiers.

CHAPTER 1

Surfing

Surfing dates all the way back to ancient Hawaii and Polynesia, more than 3,000 years ago. In this well-known sport, people use surfboards to ride along breaking waves.

Longboard and shortboard are the two main types of surfing. Longboard surfing came first. The original longboards were made out of wood. They were 8 to 10 feet (2.4 to 3 meters) long and weighed 100 pounds (45 kilograms). Although the length hasn't changed, boards today are much lighter, weighing only around 10 pounds (4.5 kg). Since they are so big, surfers have an easier time planting their feet and keeping their balance.

Shortboards are faster and easier to maneuver through the waves. They are usually 6 to 6.5 feet (1.8 to 2 m) long and weigh about 5 to 6 pounds (2.3 to 2.7 kg). Their smaller size means that they can be easily steered and used to make quick turns. Shortboards can also be faster than longboards. Today, both longboards and shortboards are made of lightweight materials, such as polyurethane and fiberglass. The have fins underneath to help surfers steer.

Usually beginner surfers start out riding longboards because they are more stable.

Many people surf for fun, but others take this sport to the extreme. They travel all over the world in search of the perfect wave. For these daring surfers, the bigger the wave, the better. An average wave is usually about 9 feet (2.7 m) tall. The biggest wave ever surfed was 78 feet (24 m) tall. The most highly sought after waves for extreme sports travel at speeds of 40 miles (64 kilometers) per hour or more.

Extreme surfers also face dangerous conditions. Some surf in extremely cold weather. Others risk drowning in the **undertow**, or getting hurt inside big waves or on rocks. And sharks are always a concern.

Extreme surfers have developed some incredible moves. They have made surfing more than just a way to conquer the waves — they have found a way to show off their grace and skill too. Popular maneuvers include tailslides, floaters, reverses, cutbacks, 360s, and airs. All these moves use the surfboard in daring and unexpected ways.

Extreme surfing can be done individually or competitively. The most **prestigious** competitions are the Vans Triple Crown of Surfing and the World Surf League Championship Tours.

undertow—an underwater current that pulls away from the shore

prestigious—having a high reputation; honored

One of surfing's biggest contests is the Titans of Mavericks Competition. The invitation-only event features 30 surfers.

surfer performing an air

SURFING MOVES

Surfing becomes truly extreme when surfers hit the waves with maneuvers that are creative, graceful, and challenging. In a tailslide, the surfer lifts the fins out of the water and slides along the wave on either the front or back of the board. A floater, where the surfer floats their board on top of a wave, requires good balance. To perform reverses and 360s, the surfer quickly changes the direction of the board. Airs are some of the most exciting tricks to watch. Both surfer and surfboard seem to leap into the air in a jump.

CHAPTER 2

Extreme Waterskiing

Waterskiing is a popular recreational activity for people of all ages. This sport involves being pulled by a boat while standing on one or two skis, which allow the skier to skim across the water. Some athletes have taken this sport from being a fun summertime activity to a truly extreme sport.

In extreme waterskiing, athletes show off their skills and take risks. They do this by racing and doing tricks. Racing depends on both the boat and the skier. Boats pull skiers at very high speeds, up to 100 miles (161 km) per hour. Skiers must then keep their balance while also battling the boat's **wake**. In slalom waterskiing, skiers have to quickly navigate a series of buoys while being pulled at around 34 miles (55 km) per hour.

Other extreme waterskiers enjoy performing tricks and stunts. They can make complete turns and do thrilling jumps off of ramps in the water. These skiers tend to use smaller skis that are easier to maneuver. Some of the most extreme waterskiers do not use skis at all, but skim over the water barefoot.

wake—the V-shaped trail of waves left behind a moving boat

Every year, waterskiers compete at the Moomba Masters in Melbourne, Australia, in trick, slalom, and jump categories.

CHAPTER 3

Extreme Board Sports

Over the years, water sports enthusiasts have found new and creative ways to use boards in the water. Surfboards are the most popular, but there are two other board sports too — wakeboarding and kitesurfing.

Wakeboarding is similar to waterskiing. It involves being pulled by a boat to travel over the water. However, instead of skis, this sport uses one wide board. A wakeboarder holds on to a rope attached to a boat. As the boat moves, the athlete uses its wake for extreme boarding.

Wakeboarding began as a combination of surfing and waterskiing. While the board might look a little bit like a surfboard, a wakeboard does not require big waves. It just needs the wake created by the boat. When a wakeboarder goes extreme, he or she performs creative tricks, stunts, and jumps. They try to get as much air as possible.

Kitesurfing, also known as kiteboarding, is similar to wakeboarding. However, instead of a boat, the athlete uses wind power to skim across the water. Kitesurfers ride on a board on the water, steering an inflatable kite. The kite attaches to a harness that the surfer wears.

Some athletes use waves for extra stunts and jumps. But even on still water, surfers can make big jumps and perform amazing tricks. All they need is the wind. In powerful winds, skilled kitesurfers can surf at nearly 58 miles (93 km) per hour.

Brad Teunissen, a wakeboarder from Australia, has competed in huge competitions, such as the Moomba Masters. His brother, Cory, is also a wakeboarder.

CHAPTER 4

Windsurfing

Following the tradition of many extreme sports, windsurfing's development borrows from other sports. In this case, it's a combination of surfing and sailing. Windsurfers, known as sailors, ride on a board that has a mast and sail attached. They use the sail to steer. Windsurfing can be a difficult sport to learn.

People first began windsurfing in the late 1950s. By the 1970s, it had become popular in North America and Europe. People wanted to show off their skills and find out who was the best. The first world championships were held in 1973. Today windsurfing is an event in the Olympic Games.

There are three main types of competitive windsurfing: freestyle, racing, and slalom. Freestyle sailors try to perform the most daring tricks. They ride huge waves and get big air when they do jumps. Racing sailors use wind power to reach top speeds. Slalom windsurfing is similar to racing, but it also involves maneuvering around obstacles.

EXTREME FACT

A racer named Antoine Albeau currently holds the record for windsurfing, with an incredible top speed of 53.27 knots — more than 61 miles (99 km) per hour.

Igor Yudakov, a 41-year-old windsurfer from Russia, is known for his extreme tricks.

CHAPTER 5

Flyboarding

Flyboarding is one of the newest and most extreme of the extreme water sports. It has only been around since 2011, but it has quickly grown in popularity. Flyboarding allows athletes to travel in and out of the water while performing jet-powered jumps and spins.

If you have never seen someone flyboarding, it might look like something out of a science-fiction movie. In this intense sport, riders wear boots with hoses that connect to a jet ski and are fastened to a board. Thanks to this jet ski power, riders can dive under the water one minute, then shoot into the air the next. A flyboard can launch a person up to 45 feet (13.7 m) into the air. It is a truly amazing experience that makes participants feel like they're part fish, part bird.

People are still learning how to make flyboards even more extreme. Right now, flyboarders perform daring tricks by shifting their weight to steer. Flyboarding is still in its early stages, so there is plenty of room for creativity.

Pioneers in flyboarding can compete in the King's Cup Thai Airways International Jet Ski World Cup.

EXTREME FACT!

The first world championships for flyboarding were held in Doha, Qatar, in 2012.

CHAPTER 6

Extreme Boating

Boating is about more than just traveling from one place to another. Kayaking and whitewater rafting require great athleticism — even more so when they're the extreme versions.

A kayak is a special type of boat that usually holds one person. The boat sits low on the water and is covered except for where the person sits in the middle. The boat's hull is rounded and the ends are curved, making it easier to navigate rough water. The kayaker uses a double-bladed paddle to steer.

Kayaking through rough waters began for practical purposes. When boating down fast rivers, people sometimes needed to travel through whitewater. This water has harsh rapids and **turbulence**. Kayaking was one of the only ways to cross safely. The thrill of whitewater kayaking inspired people to look for even more challenging ways to cross the water.

A major achievement for a kayaker is to be the first person to tackle new waters. Waterfalls are some of their favorite targets. Extreme kayakers send themselves down waterfalls higher than 100 feet (30.5 m). In order to reach this level of extreme kayaking, kayakers must have good balance, physical strength, and lots of practice under their belt.

turbulence—sudden, swirling movements in water or air

Kayakers wear safety gear, such as a helmet and a personal flotation device, in case anything goes wrong in the water.

EXTREME FACT!

In 2009, Tyler Bradt broke a world record when he kayaked over Palouse Falls in Washington. He fell 186 feet (57 m) in 3.7 seconds.

Whitewater rafting teams compete all over the world. The Pastaza River in Ecuador is know for its Class IV rapids.

Just like extreme kayaking, whitewater rafting is done on rough, turbulent waters known as rapids. Whitewater rafts are inflated and often hold multiple people. The people on the raft paddle through the rushing waters.

Rapids are categorized into six classes. Class I rapids are for beginners. They are easy to paddle through. Class VI rapids are the most difficult. Even for experts, Class VI rapids are almost impossible to navigate.

Like extreme kayakers, extreme whitewater rafters love finding new, unexplored areas to take their sport. In looking for the best undiscovered waters, they travel to some of the most beautiful places in the world, such as New Zealand, Argentina, and Colorado. Some rafters compete in slalom competitions, where they navigate through narrow gates along the rapids as fast as they can.

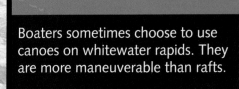

Different types of watercraft are used to tackle whitewater, including traditional inflatable rafts and sturdier canoes. The rafts are either **self-bailers** or **catarafts**. Canoes are likely to be used in the most extreme whitewater adventures.

Boaters sometimes choose to use canoes on whitewater rapids. They are more maneuverable than rafts.

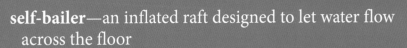

self-bailer—an inflated raft designed to let water flow across the floor

cataraft—a raft made from two inflatable tubes and a metal frame

CHAPTER 7

Extreme Free Diving

Did you ever wonder what it is like to be a mermaid or underwater creature? There is one extreme sport that comes pretty close to finding out: free diving. Free diving is like scuba diving, but without the equipment. It only requires a mask. Free divers descend into the water for minutes at a time with no oxygen tank.

Some competitive free divers dive as deep as possible on a single breath. The best free divers can hold their breath underwater for more than 10 minutes and reach depths of more than 400 feet (122 m). Other free divers also aim for deep dives, but their main goal is to connect with nature.

This sport does not have all the equipment and noise that go with other water sports. Divers can see beautiful parts of the ocean and hear what is happening underwater. However, free divers face dangers too. They might become disoriented, burst their eardrums, or lose consciousness before breaking the surface.

Free diving has existed since ancient times. However, recently, people have begun to develop new techniques. Some divers are able to slow their heart rate by up to 50 percent while diving. This helps to conserve oxygen. Free divers also have to learn how to ignore the natural reflex to breathe. Divers can get trained and certified to dive deeper and more safely.

EXTREME FACT!

Herbert Nitsch, known as "The Deepest Man on Earth," holds 33 world records in freediving.

Free diving requires lots of training, since free divers have to hold their breath in a whole new way.

CHAPTER 8

Cave Diving

Some people consider cave diving the world's most dangerous activity. While this is up for debate, there is no doubt that it has a special place in the world of extreme sports. Divers swim into the depths to explore underwater caves.

Unlike free diving, cave diving requires special equipment, such as oxygen tanks, masks, and fins. Oxygen tanks and masks allow divers to breathe underwater for long periods of time. Fins help divers to navigate the water while swimming.

Even though cave divers use equipment, this sport can be very risky. Divers explore extremely dark areas that have never been explored before. They have to prepare for every possible situation, and they have no maps to help them find their way. They must navigate the dark, winding, underwater caves, relying on their own skills.

Unlike other extreme sports, cave divers don't usually compete against each other. People who become cave divers are dedicated to the sport on a personal level. They dive in order to explore the unknown and get close to nature. Since cave diving is so dangerous, it takes years of training. The best cave divers make amazing discoveries deep in the ocean.

St. John's Cave is a popular cave diving destination in the Red Sea. It is located among the St. John's reefs.

DEEPEST CAVE

The deepest underwater cave ever reached by divers is located in the Czech Republic. It is called Hranická Propast. Krzysztof Starnawski first explored the cave in 1999. However, it wasn't until September 2016 that a Czech-Polish team, led by Starnawski, was able to explore its depths. The cave was discovered to be 1,325 feet (404 m) deep.

CHAPTER 9

Cliff Jumping

Cliff jumping is another extreme sport that doesn't require fancy or expensive equipment to participate. All you need is a cliff overlooking deep water — and a whole lot of bravery! Cliff divers jump or dive straight into the water.

This simple sport has been around for centuries. However, it became more popular thanks to high diving — a similar sport where athletes jump into water from tall platforms. Now, people look for taller and taller cliffs. Some of the best divers have jumped from cliffs 85 feet (26 m) tall. The best cliff divers participate in competitions, such as the Red Bull Cliff Diving World Series. Competitions are held in various places around the world with different **climates** and landscapes.

Even though cliff diving looks simple, it is not easy. Only the most highly trained athletes can dive from such heights. They must be in excellent shape. If a cliff diver does not enter the water properly, it can be very dangerous. The extreme heights of the cliffs mean hard impacts on the water. Cliff divers must also be careful to avoid shallow and rocky areas.

climate—the average weather of a place throughout the year

Cliff divers have hit the water at speeds of 53 to 62 miles (85 to 100 km) per hour in competitions.

CHAPTER 10

Coasteering

If you're looking for an extreme water sport that combines lots of skills, the best choice is coasteering. Coasteering involves exploring and navigating the rocky shore and the area around it. People who go coasteering are ready for whatever adventure they might find. This could mean cliff jumping, exploring caves, navigating sheer rock faces, or swimming through dangerous, choppy waters.

Coasteering was developed in Wales in the late 1900s. Like many other extreme water sports, one main goal of coasteering is exploring. People love to be close to nature and to discover brand new areas.

Anyone who wants to go coasteering must be in good physical shape. They never know what obstacles they may encounter, so they need to be ready for both the risks and rewards of climbing, swimming, diving, and any other potential challenges.

EXTREME FACT!

A specialized type of coasteering is called eco-coasteering. It allows people to get to know the natural formations of the coast and the wildlife living there.

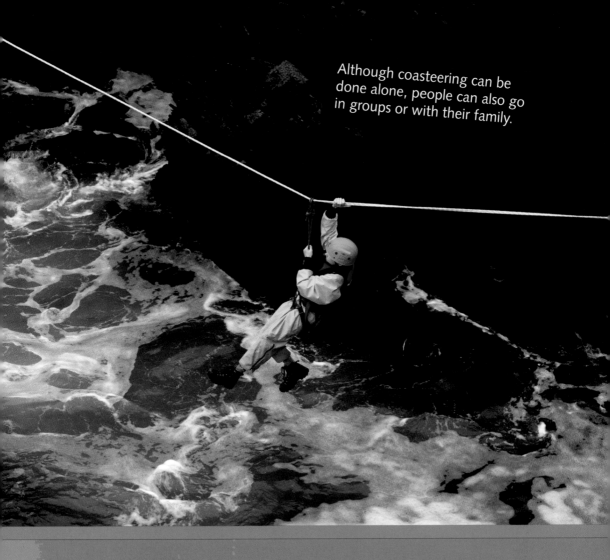

Although coasteering can be done alone, people can also go in groups or with their family.

In order to go coasteering, a person will need a wetsuit and a helmet. The wetsuit allows a person to stay warm while swimming. The helmet is used for protection in case of an accident. People usually go coasteering in groups for safety. An added benefit of coasteering in groups is exploring shorelines with others — an exhilarating activity to do with friends.

Extreme water sports make creative and daring use of one of the world's most important resources. Whether they require lots of equipment, or just the open water, they offer a huge adrenaline rush to any extreme athlete.

Glossary

cataraft (KAT-uh-raft)—a raft made from two inflatable tubes and a metal frame

climate (KLY-muht)—the average weather of a place throughout the year

prestigious (pres-TEEJ-ee-uhs)—having a high reputation; honored

self-bailer (self BAY-ler)—an inflated raft designed to let water flow across the floor

turbulence (TUR-bew-lens)—sudden, swirling movements in water or air

undertow (UN-der-tow)—an underwater current that pulls away from the shore

wake (WAYK)—the V-shaped trail of waves left behind a moving boat

Read More

Loh-Hagan, Virginia. *Extreme Cave Diving.* Nailed It! North Mankato, Minn.: 45th Parallel Press, 2016.

Luke, Andrew. *Water Sports.* Adventurous Outdoor Sports. Broomall, Penn.: Mason Crest, 2017.

Ringstad, Arnold. *Kayaking.* Great Outdoors. North Mankato, Minn.: Child's World, 2014.

Van Zee, Amy. *Bethany Hamilton: Shark Attack Survivor.* North Mankato, Minn.: Child's World, 2016.

Internet Sites

FactHound offers a safe, fun way to find Internet sites related to this book. All of the sites on FactHound have been researched by our staff.

Here's all you do:

Visit *www.facthound.com*

Type in this code: 99781515778622

Check out projects, games and lots more at
www.capstonekids.com

Index